D1312473

Diwali the magical diyas

ISBN-10: 1086343832
ISBN-13: 978-1086343830

This book belongs to:

_____

Pronunciation Guide

Ayodhya: uh - y oh dh - y ah

Diwali: d ih - w ah - l ee

Diya: d ee - y ah

Lakshmi: l uh k - sh m ee

Laxmana: lak-sh-ma na

Puja: p oo - j ah

Rama: ra-ma

Rangoli: r uh ng oh l ih

Ravana: r aa - v uh - na

Sita: s ee - t ah

Meanings

Diwali: a Hindu festival that is held in the autumn/fall, celebrated by lighting candles and clay lamps, and with fireworks.

Diya: a small oil lamp, that is shaped like a cup and made from baked clay.

Puja: a Hindu ceremony of worship.

Rangoli: a traditional Indian form of decoration consisting of patterns made with ground rice.

Exile: the condition of someone being sent or kept away from their own country.

Diwali
The Magical Diyas

Written and illustrated by
Anitha Rathod

"98, 99, 100!" exclaimed Tina as she finished counting the *diyas*.

Jay molded the clay, spun it on the potter's wheel, and declared, "And here comes our last *diya*."

Jay and Tina arranged their 101 *diyas* on the
terrace and left them to dry in the sun. "I can't
wait to light them all this *Diwali*." Tina beamed.

People clean their houses before *Diwali* to welcome Goddess *Lakshmi*.

The next day, with duster in one hand and cleaner in the other, Jay was ready to start the customary cleaning before *Diwali*. So too was Tina.

By the end of the day, their room was spick and span.

The clock struck 6, and Jay jumped to his feet and cried out, "Oh no, the play! It starts at 6." Both of them rushed to the theatre. The play was about the story of *Rama* and *Sita*.

STORY OF DIWALI

Thousands of years ago, Lord *Rama* was sent to exile, along with his wife *Sita* and brother *Laxmana*.

During the exile, *Rama* defeated the evil and most powerful ten headed demon *Ravana*.

After completing 11 years of exile and defeating *Ravana*, Lord *Rama* returned to his kingdom *Ayodhya*. The people of *Ayodhya* welcomed their king by lighting rows of clay lamps.

They lit up their homes with earthen lamps, burst crackers and decorated the whole kingdom in the most stupendous way.

And this day is celebrated by everyone with immense joy by lighting *diyas*.

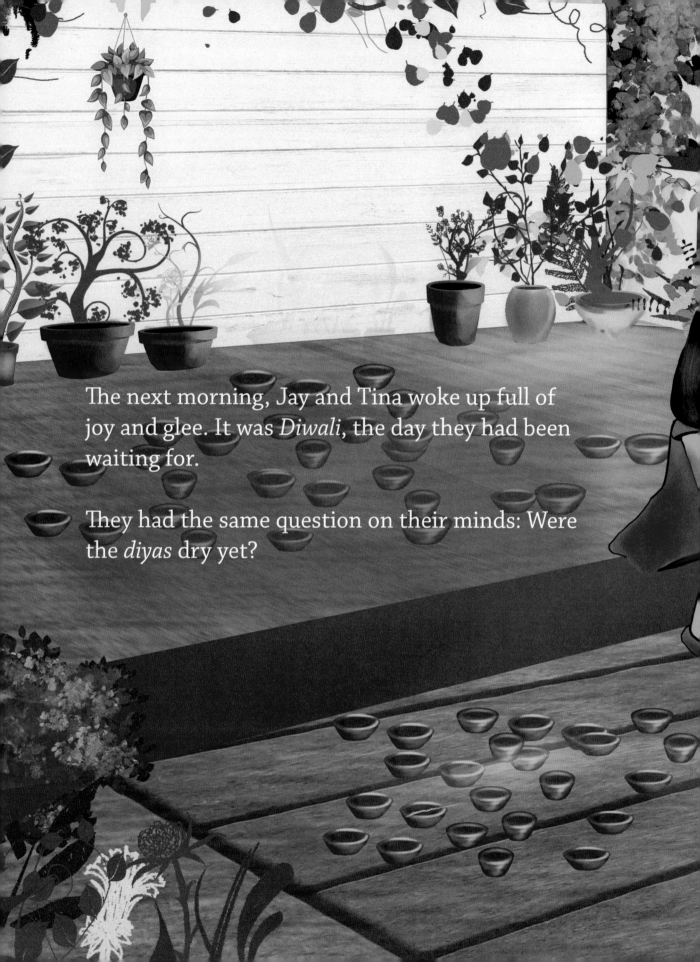

The next morning, Jay and Tina woke up full of joy and glee. It was *Diwali*, the day they had been waiting for.

They had the same question on their minds: Were the *diyas* dry yet?

They checked them all, but sadly not even one *diya* had fully dried.

"What are we going to do now?" whimpered Tina.

"Hey, come on, we have lots of other important things to do today. This is no time to be upset, it's *Diwali*," reminded Jay.

They decorated their house with beautiful marigold flowers.

Diwali decoration is incomplete without flowers and marigold flowers called 'Herb of the Sun' are considered auspicious.

"Hey, my *rangoli* design is more beautiful than yours,"
Tina teased Jay.

On *Diwali*, people decorate the floors of their living rooms and entrance of their houses, with beautiful *rangoli* designs filled with color powder.

But Jay was in no mood to give up. He added bright colors with more glitter in his *rangoli* and said, "Look now, my *rangoli* looks prettier than yours."

In the evening, Jay and Tina dressed up in their new clothes and performed *Lakshmi puja* with family members.

It was getting dark and people had already started lighting diyas in their houses, but alas, Jay and Tina had none to light.

It is believed that Goddess *Lakshmi* comes to earth on *Diwali*. People worship her for wealth and prosperity.

"For one last time, do you want to check again?" said Jay in a hopeful voice.

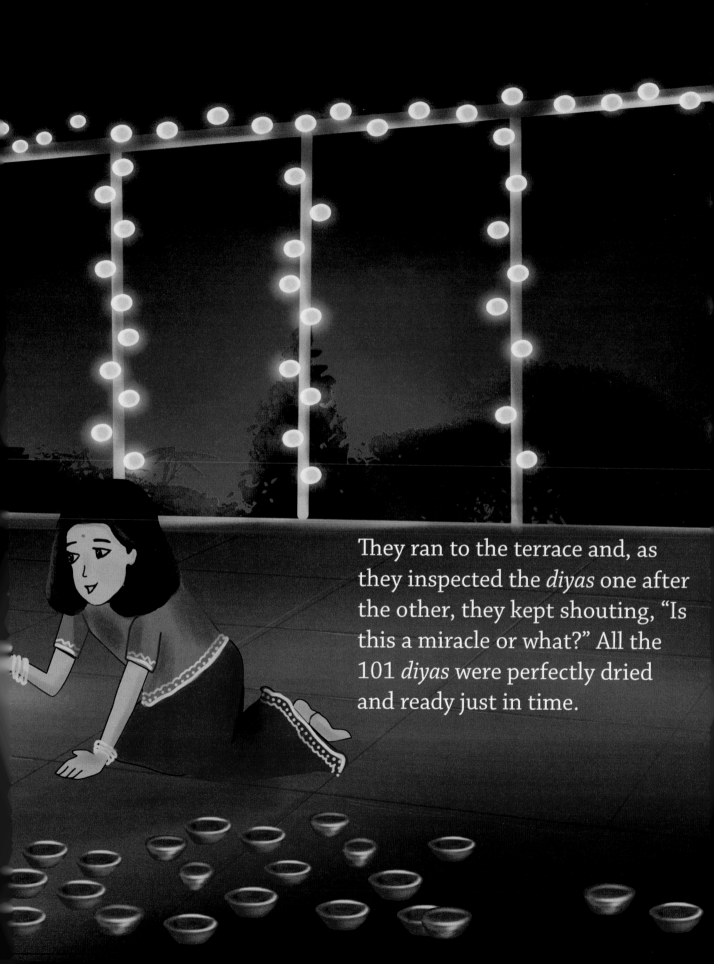

They ran to the terrace and, as they inspected the *diyas* one after the other, they kept shouting, "Is this a miracle or what?" All the 101 *diyas* were perfectly dried and ready just in time.

They lit the *diyas* and placed them at the doorsteps of every room, at the entrance, in the backyard, at the foot of the stairs, and at all other places. Their house now dazzled in the moonless night.

Jay and Tina celebrated Diwali with their family, bursting crackers and eating delicious sweets.

Diwali, also known as the 'festival of lights,' is the most important festival for all Hindus.

The festival gets its name Deepawali, or Diwali, from the rows (avali) of lamps (deepa) that the people of Ayodhya lit to welcome their King Rama.

It is a common practice to exchange gifts on Diwali.

It is the glorious occasion that is not restricted to one day but extended to a five-day celebration.

Diwali is associated with many stories and legends. One of the greatest and most famous legends behind celebrating Diwali is the victory of Lord Rama over the demon king Ravana as described in the book.

Wonder why the author kept the count of diyas as 101 and not 99, or 10 or maybe 15 or 50 or any other number for that matter?

In Hinduism, the number 101 is considered as a number of purity and hence auspicous.

About the author

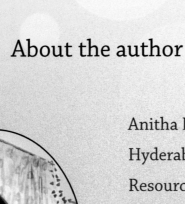

Anitha Rathod was born in the historic city of Hyderabad, India. She studied Finance and Human Resources at the Indian Institute of Management, Lucknow. She worked with corporates for about a decade before deciding to pursue her passion for writing and creating books.

She is the mother of two young and naughty kids. She loves creating books for children that are fun and filled with imagination.

Thank you for reading!

If you enjoyed reading this book, please leave an honest review on Amazon and social media. Your review will help others discover my book and encourage me to keep on writing!

I am grateful for your time and thanks for choosing to read, *"The Magical Diyas"*

Happy Diwali